## This book belongs to:

_____

_____

_____

Thank you Mom, Dad, and
my brother, Christopher, for helping
me throughout the creation of this book.
I couldn't have done it without
your love and support.

I would also like to thank Mrs. Meade,
my fourth grade teacher,
for inspiring me to the "final push"
to publish the book.

"Nothing is ever hard, just challenging!"

# The Legend

## of the

# Chocolate Cows

### Written and Illustrated
### by Frank DeGiacomo

"Well," Grandpa said, "Long ago in a far away land on a small island lived chocolate cows."

These chocolate cows were so special because they were able to make chocolate milk.

One day explorers discovered the chocolate cows on this small island and how the chocolate cows made chocolate milk!

They raced back to their King and Queen to tell them about their discovery.

The King and Queen tried the chocolate milk and thought it was the most delicious drink they had ever had.

They wanted to have their own chocolate cow, so they could have as much chocolate milk as they wanted.

The news of the chocolate cows spread throughout the kingdom so fast that everyone wanted to have their own.

Over time the chocolate cows slowly disappeared, and soon there were no more chocolate cows on the island.

Since the chocolate cows
were separated from each other,
they became very sad.

They were so sad they started producing regular milk instead of chocolate milk. Their owners got very upset.

A brilliant inventor came up with a chocolate solution that could be added to regular milk to make chocolate milk.

Since no one needed the chocolate cows anymore to make chocolate milk, everyone let them go. The chocolate cows found each other again!

They happily set off to find a new home – a place where happy chocolate cows could roam together.

"That's where chocolate milk came from, Frankie", said Grandpa. "Nowadays it's very rare to find a chocolate cow to make chocolate milk."

"That's too bad", said Frankie, "I guess it's time to go to school."

"Yes Frankie, it is time for you to go to school", said Grandpa.

CHOCOLATE MILK

MADE BY HAPPY
CHOCOLATE COWS

All chocolate cows live in a happy
and secret location where sun shines
all day and green pastures stretch for miles

The End

# CHOCOLATE MILK

## MADE BY HAPPY CHOCOLATE COWS

*All chocolate cows live in a happy and secret location where sun shines all day and green pastures stretch for miles*

# Frank D Studios

I hope you enjoyed this story
created by Frank D Studios

Check us out online at
http://frankdstudios.com
and @frankdstudios on (f) (⊚) (℗) for more!

Made in the USA
Las Vegas, NV
10 December 2024

13763115R00019